Q is for

AN ALPHABET

CLARION BOOKS

TICKNOR & FIELDS : A HOUGHTON MIFFLIN COMPANY

NEW YORK

Duck

GUESSING GAME

BY MARY ELTING
& MICHAEL FOLSOM

PICTURES BY JACK KENT

P is for Jamie and S is for Raphael

Clarion Books
Ticknor & Fields, a Houghton Mifflin Company

Printed in the United States of America

Library of Congress Cataloging in Publication Data

Elting, Mary, 1906-   Q is for duck.
Summary: While learning some facts about animals, the
reader is challenged to guess why A is for zoo, B is for dog,
and C is for hen.
[1. Alphabet. 2. Animals] I. Folsom, Michael, joint author.
II. Kent, Jack, 1920-   III. Title.
PZ7.E53Qab   [E]   80-13854
RNF ISBN 0-395-29437-1   PAP ISBN 0-395-30062-2

Y 10 9 8 7 6 5 4

A is for Zoo

Why?

Because...

Animals live in the Zoo

B is for Dog

Why?

Because a Dog **B**arks

C is for Hen

Why?

Because a Hen Clucks

D is for Mole

Why?

Because a Mole Digs

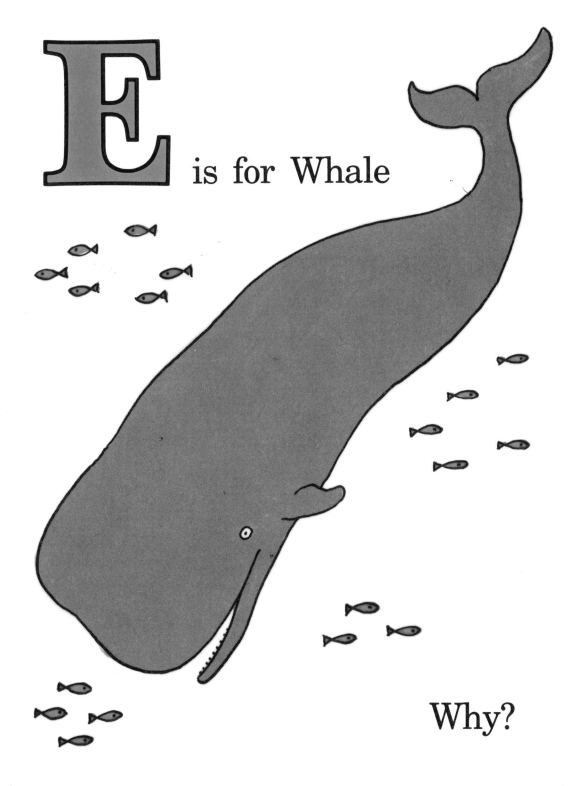

E is for Whale

Why?

Because…

a Whale is Enormous

F is for Bird

Why?

Because a Bird **F**lies

G is for Horse

Why?

Because a Horse Gallops

H is for Owl

Why?

Because an Owl **H**oots

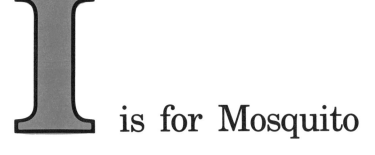

I is for Mosquito

Why?

Because
Mosquito bites Itch

J is for Kangaroo

Why?

Because a Kangaroo **J**umps

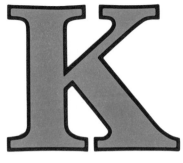 **K** is for Mule

Why?

Because a Mule **K**icks

L is for Frog

Why?

Because a Frog **L**eaps

M is for Cow

Why?

Because a Cow **M**oos

 is for Cat

Why?

Because a Cat Naps

O

is for Pig

Why?

Because a Pig Oinks

P is for Chick

Why?

Because a Chick Peeps

Q is for Duck

Why?

Because a Duck **Q**uacks

R

is for Lion

Why?

ROAR

Because a Lion **R**oars

S is for Camel

Why?

Because a Camel Spits

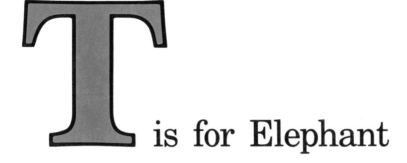

T is for Elephant

Why?

Because
an Elephant Trumpets

U is for Prairie Dog

Why?

Because Prairie Dogs live

Underground

V is for Chameleon

Why?

Because a
Chameleon seems to Vanish

 is for Snake

Why?

Because a Snake **W**iggles

 **X** is for Dinosaur

Why?

Because Dinosaurs are

e**X**tinct

Y is for Coyote

Why?

Because a Coyote **Y**owls

Z is for Animals

Why?

Because
Animals live in the Zoo